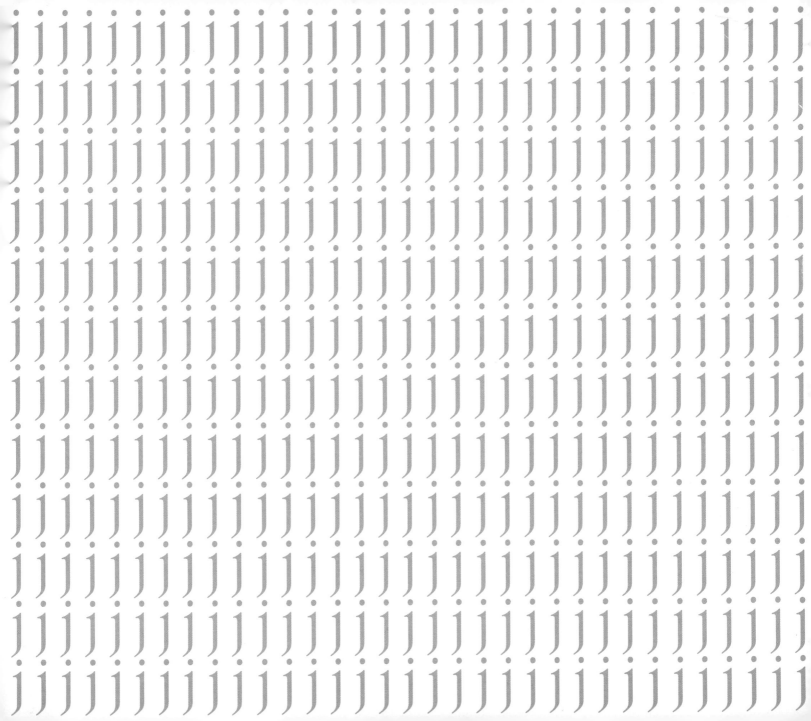

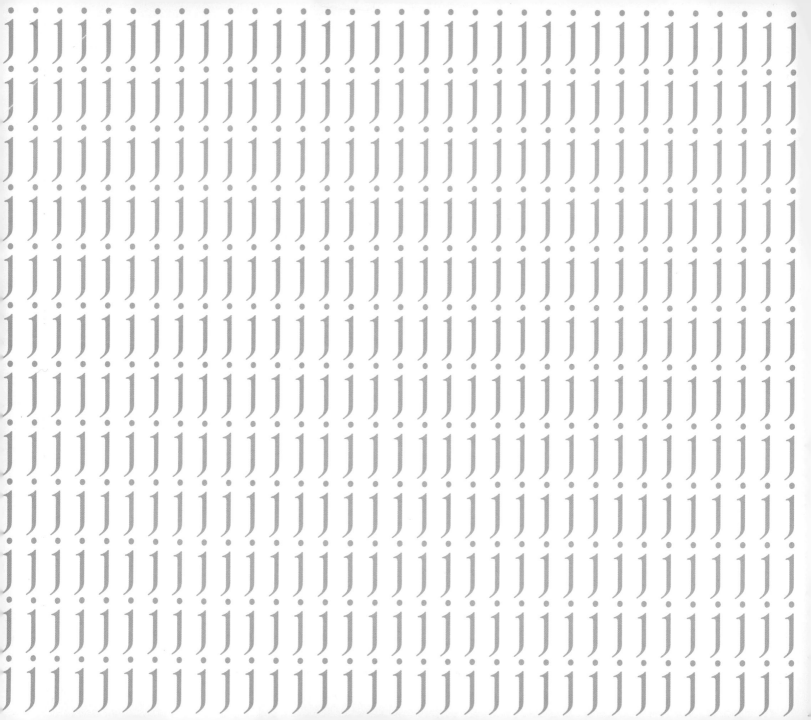

My "j" Sound Box®

Library of Congress Cataloging-in-Publication Data
Moncure, Jane Belk.
My "j" sound box / by Jane Belk Moncure; illustrated by Colin King
p. cm.
Summary: A little boy fills his sound box with many words beginning with the letter "j."
ISBN 1-56766-776-7 (lib. bdg. : alk. paper)
[1. Alphabet.] I. King, Colin, ill. II. Title.
PZ7.M739 Myj 2000
[E]—dc21   99-055420

My "j"
Sound Box

Jane Belk Moncure

illustrated by Colin King

The Child's World

Little  had a box.

"I will find things that begin with my 'j' sound," he said.

"I will put them into

my sound 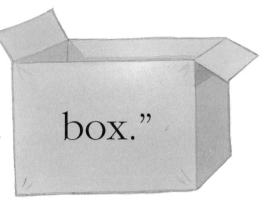 box."

But first, Little 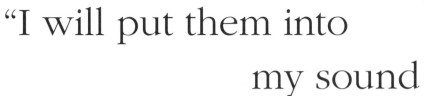 put on

his jeans and  jacket.

"I will jump," he said.

He jumped over the box
like a jumping jack.

Then he jumped  into the box.

"I am a jack-in-the-box!" he said.
He jumped up.

Little jumped up a hill.

"I will jump like Jack and Jill," he said.

He jumped down the hill.
Then he saw a . . .

 jack-o'-lantern.

Did he put the
jack-o'-lantern into
his box? He did.

Then Little J jumped until he saw . . .

jackrabbits!

Jumping jackrabbits.

Did he put the jumping jackrabbits into the box with the jack-o'-lantern? He did.

Then he jumped until he saw . . .

jays.

The jays cried, "Jay, jay, jay!"

Little  put them into the box with the jack-o'-lantern and the jackrabbits.

Now the box was full, so . . .

Little  found a jeep.

He put the box with the jackrabbits,
jays, and jack-o'-lantern into the jeep . . .

and drove into the jungle.

Just then, Little saw a jaguar.

The jaguar was about to jump
on the jackrabbits!

Little held up the
jack-o'-lantern and . . .

the jaguar jumped away!

Little  caught the jaguar.

He took him to jail

so he could not jump on the jackrabbits.

Just then,

Little j saw Jumbo,

the jolly elephant.

"Jumbo is too big for my sound box," he said.

Little  found a jet. A jumbo jet! It was big enough for the animals and everything else.

Jumbo

jackrabbits

jumbo jet

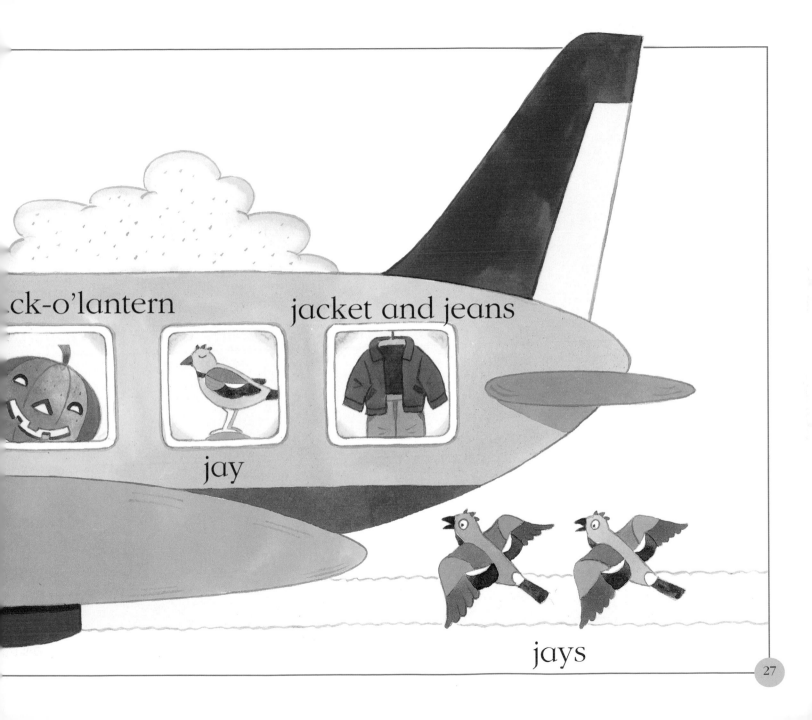

ck-o'lantern

jacket and jeans

jay

jays

Can you read these words with Little ?

jar

jonquil

jacks

jade

jellyfish

jewelry

jackal

January

1	2	3	4	5	6	7
8	9	10	11	12	13	14
15	16	17	18	19	20	21
22	23	24	25	26	27	28
29	30	31				

June

				1	2	3
4	5	6	7	8	9	10
11	12	13	14	15	16	17
18	19	20	21	22	23	24
25	26	27	28	29	30	

July

						1
2	3	4	5	6	7	8
9	10	11	12	13	14	15
16	17	18	19	20	21	22
23	24	25	26	27	28	

juggler

jelly

juice

ABOUT THE AUTHOR AND ILLUSTRATOR

Jane Belk Moncure began her writing career when she was in kindergarten. She has never stopped writing. Many of her children's stories and poems have been published, to the delight of young readers, including her son Jim, whose childhood experiences found their way into many of her books.

Mrs. Moncure's writing is based upon an active career in early childhood education.
A recipient of an M.A. degree from Columbia University, Mrs. Moncure has taught and directed nursery, kindergarten, and primary grade programs in California, New York, Virginia, and North Carolina. As a former member of the faculties of Virginia Commonwealth University and the University of Richmond, she taught prospective teachers in early childhood education.

Mrs. Moncure has travelled extensively abroad, studying early childhood programs in the United Kingdom, The Netherlands, and Switzerland. She was the first president of the Virginia Association for Early Childhood Education and received its award for outstanding service to young children.

A resident of North Carolina, Mrs. Moncure is currently a full-time writer and educational consultant. She is married to Dr. James A. Moncure, former vice president of Elon College.

Colin King studied at the Royal College of Art, London. He started his freelance career as an illustrator, working for magazines and advertising agencies.

He began drawing pictures for children's books in 1976 and has illustrated over sixty titles to date.

Included in a wide variety of subjects are a best-selling children's encyclopedia and books about spies and detectives.

His books have been translated into several languages, including Japanese and Hebrew. He has four grown-up children and lives in Suffolk, England, with his wife, three dogs, and a cat.

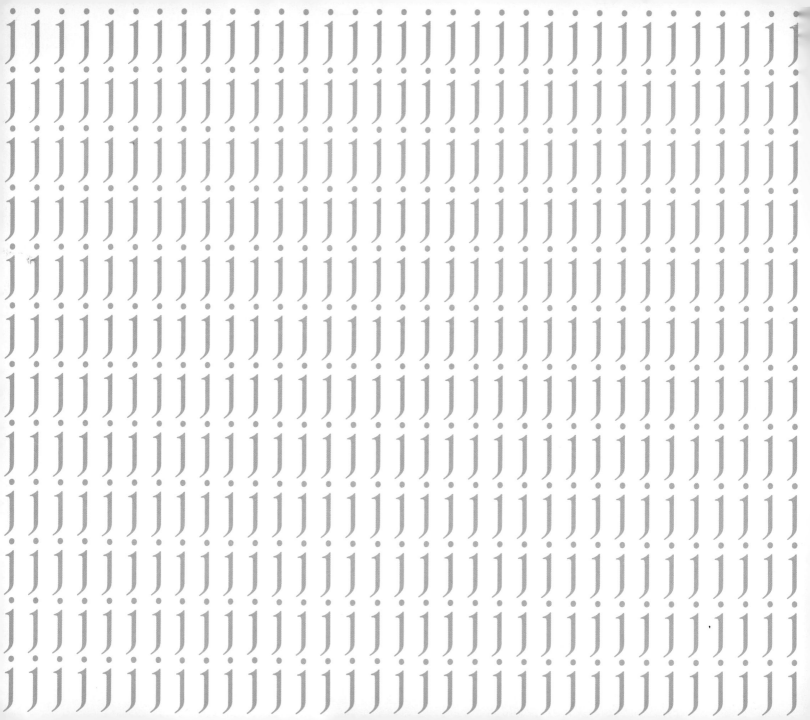